Library of Congress Cataloging-in-Publication Data
Names: Singleton, Linda Joy, author. Smythe, Richard, illustrator. • Title: Crane & crane /
by Linda Joy Singleton; illustrated by Richard Smythe. • Other titles: Crane and crane
Description: Mankato, MN: Amicus Ink is published by Amicus, [2019] • Summary:
Illustrations and simple text show the parallels between a pair of sandhill cranes
building a nest and a construction crane being used to build a cabin for a
family. • Identifiers: LCCN 2018021665 ISBN 9781681524085
(hardcover: alk. paper) • Subjects: | CYAC: Cranes, derricks, etc.
—Fiction. | Cranes (Birds)—Fiction. Sandhill crane—Fiction. |
House construction—Fiction. Building—Fiction. | Birds—
Nests—Fiction. Classification: LCC PZ7.S6177
Cr 2019 | DDC [E]—dc23 • LC record available
at https://lccn.loc.gov/2018021665

First edition 9 8 7 6 5 4 3 2 1
Printed in China

For my Jurga.—R.S.

To my husband David, who was a crane operator for thirty
years. I couldn't have done this book without him.—L.J.S.

CRANE & CRANE

by Linda Joy Singleton
illustrated by Richard Smythe

amicus ink

Mankato, Minnesota

Lift.

Lift.

Stretch.

Stretch.

Honk.

Grab.

Grab.

Glide.

Glide.

Stack.

Stack.

Swoosh.

Swoosh.

Pick.

Pick.

Sway.

Thump.

Thump.

Plop.

Plop.

Crack.

Clack.

Peep.

Sleep.

Home.

CRANE vs. CRANE

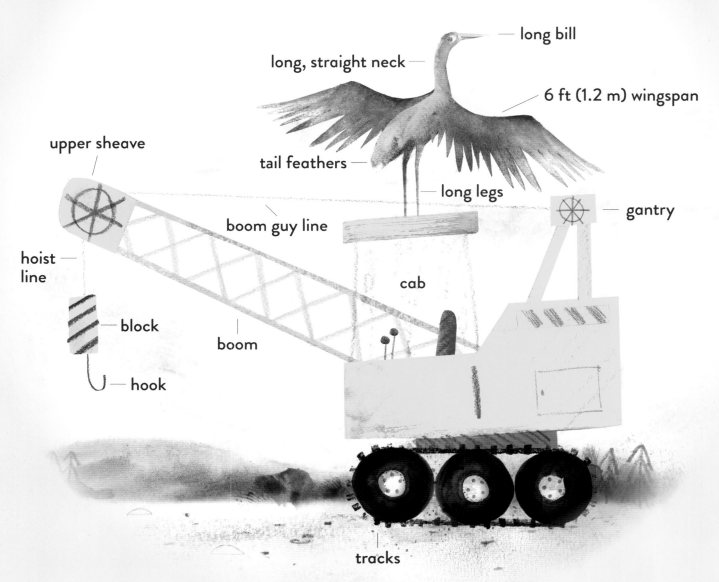

long bill

long, straight neck

6 ft (1.2 m) wingspan

tail feathers

long legs

upper sheave

gantry

boom guy line

hoist line

cab

block

boom

hook

tracks